The First Snow

DAVID CHRISTIANA

SCHOLASTIC PRESS

NEW YORK

Library of Congress Cataloging-in-Publication Data
Christiana, David.
The first snow / by David Christiana.
p.   cm.
Summary: Winter seeks acceptance from the young Mother Nature,
who hates the season and tries to keep it away by painting
the trees bright and wild colors.
ISBN 0-590-22855-2
[1. Winter — Fiction. 2. Snow — Fiction.] I. Title.
PZ7.C452844Fi   1996   95-25062
CIP   AC
12 11 10 9 8 7 6 5 4 3 2 1   6 7 8 9/9 0 1/0
Printed in the United States of America   37
First printing, October 1996

The illustrations in this book were executed with graphite pencil and watercolor,
along with a touch of gouache, on Strathmore Bristol and paper that was left in a barn
near Washington Crossing, Pennsylvania.
The text type was set in Veljovic Book by WLCR, New York, NY.
The display type was hand-lettered by Jeanyee Wong.

For Mother Nature's Children

Long ago

in the time of two seasons,
Mother Nature was a little girl
who only liked warm weather.

"I hate Winter," she would say. "And that
friend of his, The Wind, is a monster."

But like it or not, a cold crisp morning always arrived
with the smell of something chilly on the leaves.
"Here they come again," the girl would complain.

One day, she even asked Summer to stay with her forever.

"I'm afraid that would be impossible," Summer told the little girl. She packed her trunk full of warm and green breezes. It was time to go.

The little girl frowned. She asked her favorite tree, "Do you like Winter? You look so bare and gray when The Wind takes your leaves."

"Actually, I look forward to a bit of rest," whispered the tree.

"Well, I don't," replied the girl. Hoping to scare
away Winter and his friend, The Wind, she painted
the leaves bright, wild colors.

When Winter arrived, he was shocked. "Fire-colored
trees? I've never seen such a thing!" He turned around
in a huff and rode The Wind away.

Winter was still upset when he got home.
He asked Aunt Arctica, "Why doesn't the little girl
like me? What's so pleasing about Summer?"
"She has her days," said Aunt Arctica.
"What about *my* days?" asked Winter.

"Hush," ordered Aunt Arctica. "The little girl just
needs to get to know you better. When you next see her,
you must be brave." She sent Winter and The Wind
on their way again.

Winter took Aunt Arctica's advice. "Charge!"
The Wind howled more loudly than he ever had before.

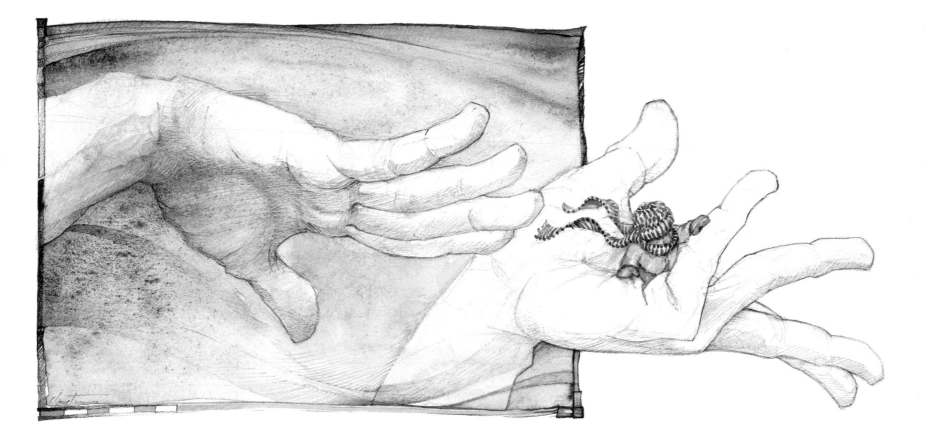

The trees shook and shivered, but the little girl did
not. She painted a mask and dressed up as a beast to
scare away Winter and his friend.

Back home again, Winter wondered what to do.
"She's a tough one," said Aunt Arctica. "Perhaps
there's a better way."

The next morning, Winter snuck up on the girl
and sent a flock of goosebumps tingling up her arm.
"I hate goosebumps!" the little girl said. "Winter, go
away! And take that monstrous Wind with you."

So Winter stayed away
that year and Summer
unpacked. The warmth
continued. The trees
kept growing...

...and growing.

But Aunt Arctica knew that every season
must have its turn. "Try a gentler approach,"
she told Winter.

Winter sang a lullaby to the little girl.

The leaves were enchanted and danced to the ground.

They covered the little girl,
but she didn't seem to mind.

Winter called out, "Little girl, where are you?"

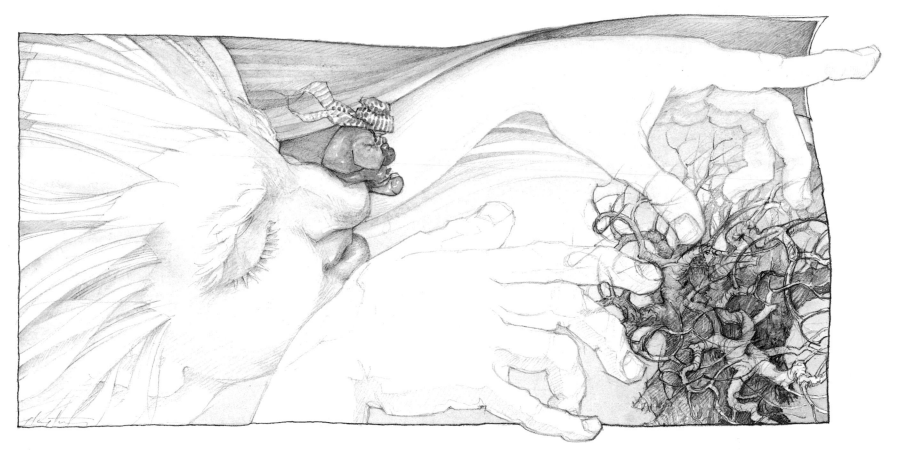

The little girl stayed hidden. *It's Winter again.*
He doesn't frighten me at all. This time, she thought,
I will scare him to death.

But when the little girl jumped and shouted,
she was frozen through and through.

It had never been so cold.

Now, you might think that Winter would have been delighted, but he wasn't. He had grown fond of the little girl. He made a blanket from the softest white crystals...

... that fell from the sky like angels' tears.

When he wrapped the blanket around the little girl,
she awoke, and her coldness went away.

Winter had arrived, and the world
all around was beautiful.

It was the first snow.